For Everette,
May you always find wonder in nature
—L. L.

To Taylor who served enthusiastically as the model for Henry, and in memory
of his loving father, Michael "Howie" Mandell
—J. L.

With special thanks to the #502 writers for reading drafts and offering your insights; to
Ryan Ammons, who shared a childhood memory that planted the seed for this story; and to Mark
Hardy, my writing buddy, for your honest feedback and for confirming details with beekeeper
friends. And with eternal gratitude to Steve, for your loving support and unflagging belief in me.

Published by
PEACHTREE PUBLISHERS
1700 Chattahoochee Avenue
Atlanta, Georgia 30318-2112
www.peachtree-online.com

Text © 2018 by Lester L. Laminack
Illustrations © 2018 by Jim LaMarche

Edited by Margaret Quinlin and Vicky Holifield
Design and composition by Nicola Simmonds Carmack
Production supervision by Melanie McMahon Ives

The publisher wishes to thank Jeff Gold for his invaluable assistance with beekeeping details.

The illustrations were rendered in ink and watercolor.

Printed in September 2017 by Tien Wah Press in Malaysia
10 9 8 7 6 5 4 3 2 1
First Edition
HC: 978-1-56145-953-7

Library of Congress Cataloging-in-Publication Data

Names: Laminack, Lester L., 1956- author. | LaMarche, Jim, illustrator.
Title: The king of bees / written by Lester L. Laminack ; illustrated by Jim LaMarche.
Description: First edition. | Atlanta, Georgia : Peachtree Publishers, [2018] | Summary: Henry is
fascinated by the bees his Aunt Lilla cares for and he would love to help, but she says he must
wait until he is older.
Identifiers: LCCN 2017022430 | ISBN 9781561459537
Subjects: | CYAC: Beekeeping—Fiction. | Bees—Fiction. | Aunts—Fiction.
Classification: LCC PZ7.L1815 Kin 2018 | DDC [E]—dc23 LC record available at https://lccn.loc.
gov/2017022430

The King of Bees

Lester L. Laminack

Illustrated by Jim LaMarche

PEACHTREE
ATLANTA

Henry and Aunt Lilla lived deep in the Lowcountry, where South Carolina reaches out and mingles with the saltwater to form tidal creeks and marshes. Sometimes Henry felt like the whole world ended at the far edge of that water.

Their small wooden house had a tucked-in porch and a ghost of white paint. Out back there was a vegetable garden, a hen house, an old shed, and—Henry's favorite— the beehives. He felt something special for the bees.

Henry could hardly wait to help with the bees. Aunt Lilla finally agreed that he could watch her check the hive boxes. He waited eagerly at the door of the shed as she stepped into her bee suit and put on the hat with the net that protected her face. She let Henry carry the smoker she used to calm the bees.

"A bee won't sting you unless you get in the way of what she's doing," Aunt Lilla told him as they made their way to the hives. "But you got to stay a good ways back for now," she warned. "Climb up on that stump while I'm working and you'll see everything just fine."

Aunt Lilla spoke softly while she lifted the frames to see how the bees were doing.

"What are you saying to them?" Henry asked.

"I'm just giving 'em a little encouragement." She spoke louder to be sure he could hear her. "You girls are busy fanning this morning. Got to get that honey ready, don't you?"

Henry listened to the bees. "Aunt Lilla," he called,
"When the bees hum are they talking back to you?"

"No, Henry. Sister bees hum when they're working. If
they have news to tell, they do their talking-dance. That's
how a bee shows her sisters where to find the best flowers."

"How come you always talk about the sister bees?"
Henry asked her. "Don't they have any
brother bees?" Aunt Lilla chuckled.
"Well, sir, there are a few boy bees to
mate with the queen. They don't
do much else, except eat."

For weeks Henry pestered Aunt Lilla about helping with the hives. "There's plenty of time for that," she said. "You got some growing to do first."

He would have to be patient because Aunt Lilla was particular about certain things.

Henry remembered when she let him gather eggs from the henhouse all by himself. That first day he'd tried to take too many at a time and dropped one.

Aunt Lilla wasn't upset, but her voice was serious. "You got to be extra careful, Henry. Those eggs are food and money for us."

He'd learned quickly how to slip the eggs from the nests. Now he enjoyed gathering them every day.

One morning, Henry decided to explore the shed where Aunt Lilla kept her bee-keeping tools. He examined the uncapping fork and the hive tool. He touched the smoker. He opened the bottle of bee drops and sniffed them. Aunt Lilla had told him how much the bees liked the smell.

His eyes came to rest on the bee suit. He was certain there was something magic about it. He just knew if he had one of his own he could get closer to the hives and bee-talk like Aunt Lilla.

Henry left the shed and found Aunt Lilla in the garden. "How come the brother bees don't help their sisters?" he asked. "Can't the king bee make them do some of the work?"

"Well, Henry," she said, "the hive's like a big busy family that's got one queen and a whole bunch of sisters. The sister bees clean the hive and bring in nectar and pollen to feed all the bees. They make the honey and take care of the queen, too."

"They don't have a king?" he asked.

"No, I reckon the bee family gets along just fine with only a queen."

Henry thought about this. "Aunt Lilla, it's not right for the sisters to do all the work. If I was a bee I'd do a lot to help my sisters. Just like I help you with the hens and the garden."

Day after day, Henry watched the sister bees buzzing in and out of the hive boxes. Henry imagined the bees doing their talking-dance inside the hive, telling all the other sisters where to find new flowers.

One morning Henry jumped off his stump and did a little dance of his own. He was telling his bees how to find the big patch of clover blooming on the backside of Mr. Craven's pasture. When he hummed and danced, Henry *was* a bee.

He knew this for sure and certain when he saw sister bees buzzing in that clover patch the next day.

Before long, Henry noticed a lot of activity around the hives. Aunt Lilla noticed, too. "Looks like the bees are fixing to swarm," she said. "I suspect we're about to get a new queen."

"What's going to happen to our queen, Aunt Lilla?" Henry asked.

"The old queen will fly off with a bunch of the sisters and search for a new spot to make another hive," she said.

"Will they really try to leave us?" Henry asked.

"They could. We got to do all we can to keep 'em here, Henry. We depend on that honey about as much as those bees do."

More and more sister bees flew out and circled the hives.

"I best hurry," she said. "I'll set up another box over by the tupelo tree."

Henry wanted to do something
to help. Maybe he could tell the bees
where to find the new box? But he'd
have to get closer to the hives.

He went into the shed, lifted
Aunt Lilla's bee suit off the peg, and
stepped into it. He pushed up the long
sleeves and pulled up the legs until
he could see his shoes.

As he reached for the hat, he
tipped over the bottle of bee drops
and some of the liquid spilled out.
Henry put the lid back on the bottle
and returned it to the shelf. Then he
wiped his hands on the bee suit and
stumbled out of the shed.

That too-big bee suit made it hard to walk, but Henry was determined to let the bees know about the new box.

He shuffled past the watching stump. This was the closest he had ever been to the hive boxes. Sister bees were buzzing in and out like never before, and the hum made his skin tingle.

He stood still and listened. The sound of it got inside of him.

Slowly he began to move, careful not to trip. He danced to tell the bees they didn't have to leave.

Dancing in that bulky bee suit made Henry so tired he had to go rest awhile. He trudged across the yard, dragging it behind him like a shadow. He didn't notice the bees following him.

Henry climbed the porch steps and stretched out on the bench. A low buzz caught his attention. He lay perfectly still and watched as the swarm of bees settled on the bee suit.

When Aunt Lilla came onto the porch, she stopped on the top step.

"Henry?" she called softly.

"Look, Aunt Lilla!" he said. "The sister bees decided to stay."

"Don't move," she whispered. "I'll run fetch the smoker. Just to be safe."

Henry hummed softly.

A few minutes later, Aunt Lilla returned
with the smoker. She puffed clouds of white
smoke over the bees, then carefully lifted
the bee suit from Henry's legs and carried
it away.

When Aunt Lilla came back, she said, "I set the bee suit down by the box and the bees went right for it."

She pulled Henry close. "I'm proud of you, Henry."

"The bees were leaving, Aunt Lilla. I had to tell them about the new box."

"Were you scared when all those bees were on you?" she asked.

"No ma'am. I can bee-talk now, just like you." he said. "They came to say thank you because I was a helpful brother bee."

Henry looked out toward the hives. "Aunt Lilla, those bees will stay with us, I just know it. I reckon they think I'm their king bee."

Aunt Lilla smiled and said, "And I reckon you'll be a good one, too."

Author's Note

When I was a boy I loved to visit my grandmother's house. Like Henry's Aunt Lilla, she was patient and gentle, and she was never in a hurry. She introduced me to the magic of working with the flowers and vegetables in her small garden. She was not a beekeeper, but she respected the bees and taught me how the pollination of flowers and vegetables depended on the honeybees.

Ever since then, honeybees have held a special magic for me. Everything about them fills me with wonder. These tiny creatures make honey from the nectar of flowers. They build a hive filled with perfectly uniform hexagonal cells. They communicate essential information about where to find nectar and pollen through a specialized dance. Every member of the hive has an essential function and an uncanny focus for work. They work together and are willing to die to protect the hive and save their queen.

Every time I learn a new fact about honeybees, I am even more amazed at just how incredible they are. Did you know that a worker bee will spend her life gathering nectar and pollen for the colony? And did you know that producing one teaspoon of honey takes the combined efforts of twelve worker bees for the entirety of their short lifetimes? Well, it does. One worker bee will visit fifty to one hundred flowers in a single trip and as many as two thousand flowers in one day! Bees are indeed busy!

And that's not all. While they are out foraging for their colony, they move from flower to flower pollinating the plants that produce much of the food we eat. By some reports, as much as one-third of our food comes from honeybee pollination.

Like Henry, I am fascinated with honeybees and I believe that we need to work together to keep them healthy. We need to pay attention to the threats to their existence, like loss of their habitat, use of pesticides that damage their hives, and climate changes that impact the blooming season of plants they depend upon. I hope you'll join me in an effort to help protect honeybees in our daily lives. For more information and resources about these magical creatures, please visit *www.peachtree-online.com/honeybees.*

Lester Laminack